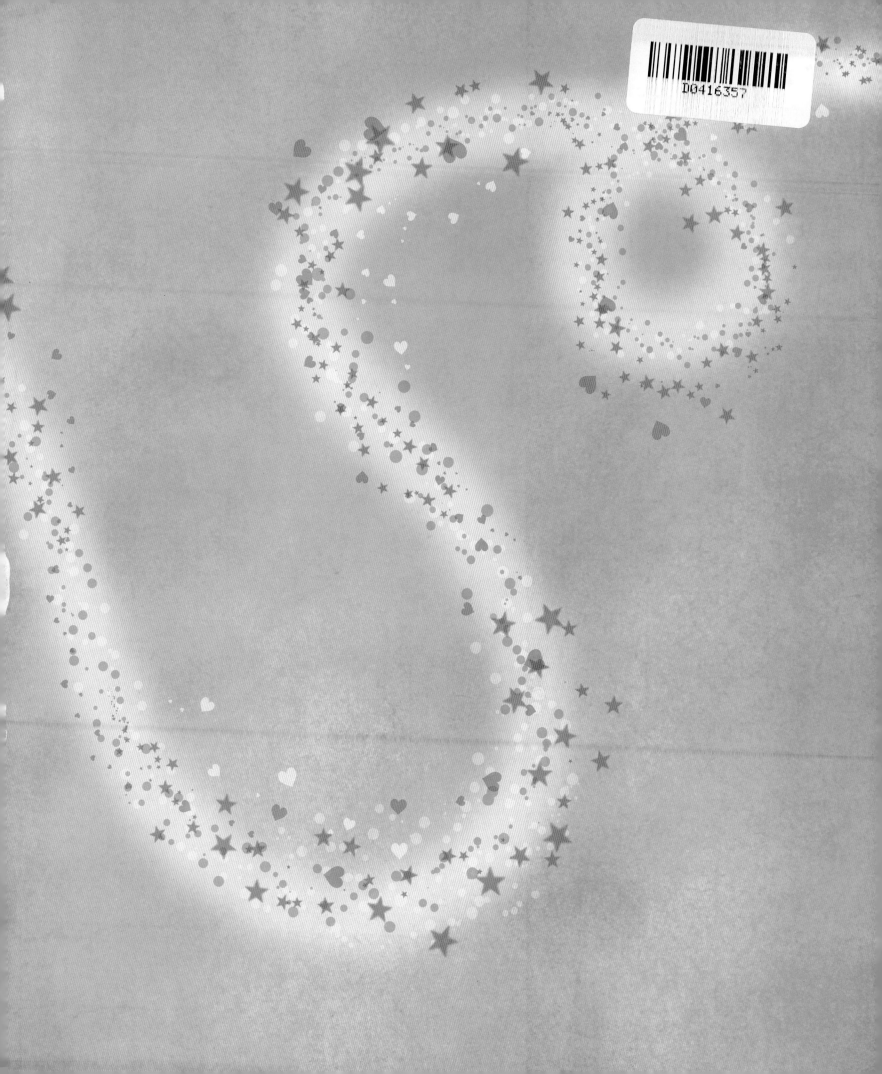

This edition published by Parragon Books Ltd in 2014

Parragon Books Ltd, Chartist House, 15–17 Trim Street, Bath BA1 1HA, UK

www.parragon.com   Copyright © Parragon Books Ltd 2013

Designed by Claire Brisley and Duck Egg Blue

Production by Richard Wheeler

Edited by Lily Holland and Becky Wilson

ISBN 978-1-4723-4929-3   Printed in China

Pinkabella

and the Fairy Goldmother

Pinkabella™

and the Fairy Goldmother

Written by
Gillian Rogerson

Illustrated by
Bruno Merz

PaRRagon

Bath · New York · Cologne · Melbourne · Delhi
Hong Kong · Shenzhen · Singapore · Amsterdam

Pinkabella's godmother was coming to stay!
"Hello, Auntie Alura!" cried Pinkabella, excitedly. She threw
herself into her godmother's arms and nearly knocked her over.

"Whoa, steady! Now, let me look at you," Auntie Alura smiled. "You've grown so much. Do you still think I'm your fairy godmother?"

Pinkabella nodded and pointed to her godmother's dress. "You're always so glittery!"

Auntie Alura laughed. "Maybe I'm your fairy **gold**mother... You know I love gold almost as much as you love pink!"

"You're sleeping in my room," Pinkabella told her auntie,
"and I'm staying with Ned and Ted."

"Ah, double trouble," Auntie Alura teased,
reaching for a cuddle with the twins.

Auntie Alura smiled when she saw Pinkabella's room, "It's very..."

"Pinktastic!"
beamed Pinkabella.

"Pinkerrific!"
Violet added.

"Yes, and I see you've tidied up," said Auntie Alura.

"Come on, Violet," said Pinkabella. "Let's take some of my things to Ned and Ted's room."

"Hmm," said Pinkabella,
when they got to Ned and Ted's room,
"I'm missing something..."

My favourite
pink PJs!

"My pinktacular room has gone!" cried Pinkabella.

"Auntie Alura has goldified it!"

"But how did she do that?" asked Violet. Suddenly, Pinkabella saw a sparkly stick on the end of her bed...

"It looks like a wand," said Pinkabella.
"Do you think it's magic?" asked Violet.
Pinkabella grabbed the stick. "Let's try it!"

She waved the wand and said,

"Make everything
pinktastic!"

Suddenly the stick made a fizzing noise
and pink sparkles shot out of the end...

The sparkles whizzed through the air,

and everything they landed on

turned *bright pink.*

"Wow, it IS real! Let's take turns!" said Violet, stretching out one hand.

Pinkabella threw the wand to Violet, but it whizzed over her friend's head, bounced off the wall and zoomed back towards Pinkabella.

"Aargh!" cried Pinkabella, ducking down, and the wand flew out of the open window.

Pinkabella and Violet watched in horror as the wand twirled away, shooting pink sparkles everywhere it went.

Down it spiralled towards the garden...

and Pinkabella's family!

Pinkabella and Violet ran into the garden.

"I'm really sorry, Auntie Alura!" Pinkabella began. "I didn't know your wand was real. I just wanted my room pink again!"

"It's okay, I'm sorry too," Auntie Alura smiled at Pinkabella. "I shouldn't have made your room gold without asking you. Now, let's get everything back to normal."

Dad smiled, "So one of you loves pink and one of you loves gold. What are you going to do?"

"I've got an idea. Can I borrow your wand, Auntie Alura?" asked Pinkabella.

"Pink and gold together... I love it!" Auntie Alura beamed.
Pinkabella twirled around.

The End

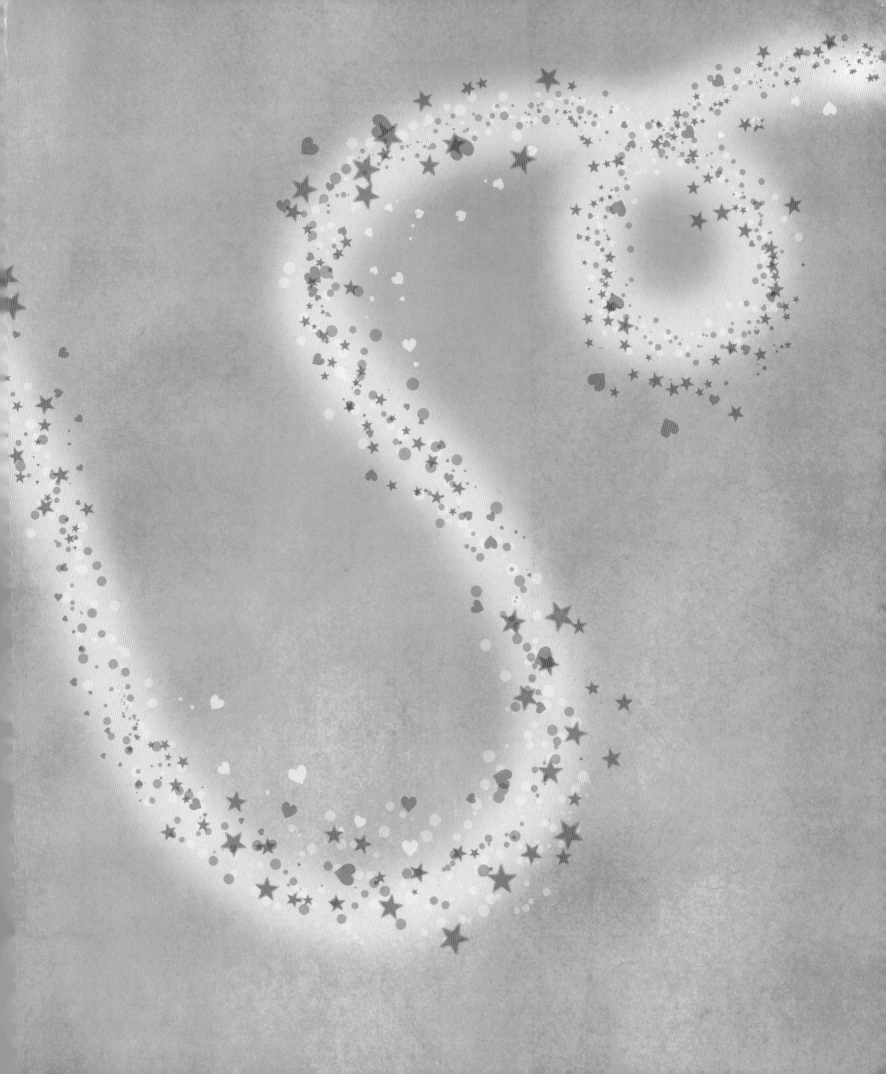